W9-ABG-248

Charles E. Martin

SAM SAVES THE DAY

Greenwillow Books, New York

Printed in Singapore by Tien Wah

First Edition 1 2 3 4 5 6 7 8 9 10

Watercolors and ink were used for the full-color
illustrations. The text type is Goudy Old Style.

Library of Congress Cataloging-in-Publication Data

Martin, Charles E., (date)
Sam saves the day.
Summary: Sam has a busy summer—first
traveling, then helping his neighbor take
in his lobster traps, and finally helping
his island baseball team win a game.
[1. Summer—Fiction] I. Title.
PZ7.M356777Sam 1987 [E] 86-19594
ISBN 0-688-06814-6
ISBN 0-688-06815-4 (lib. bdg.)

FOR DOUG AND HARRY

The first day of summer vacation Mrs. Gray called the school together. "Baseball season starts next week," she said. "Our field is a mess. We'll all have to work hard to fix it up." Everyone promised to help. But Sam found out his mother and father had other plans for him.

Aunt Kate was getting married, and they were going to the wedding in Arizona. On the way back they would do some sight-seeing. And while they were gone, Mr. Stanley would get Dad's boat in shape for a busy summer of fishing parties.

Sam's friends came to the dock to wave him off.

Everyone had a good time at the wedding. They all said they had never seen Aunt Kate look so beautiful. The next day Sam and his parents left for the Grand Canyon.

"Grand is the right word for it," Mom said. They all agreed.

They went to a rodeo. They spent a day in the desert looking into ancient caves. They visited some Indian villages.

"It makes you not want to go home," Dad said.

But like all vacations, it had to end. Their neighbor Alfred was at the dock to take them back to the island. He told them he would be fined unless he got his lobster traps in by Monday, and his helper had sprained his ankle.

Sam offered to do the job.

"Great," Alfred said. "We're off first thing in the morning."

Sam's mother woke him up at sunrise.

On his way to work, Sam met Mrs. Gray, who was out jogging.

"I'm glad to see you're back," she said. "The field is ready and we're having our first game with Port Hyde on Monday. We have three good summer-visitor players, but we're weak on pitching. We need you."

Sam told her he had promised to help Alfred, but the traps would be in by Monday so he could play.

Sam felt badly about not being at practice, but out on the water there was no doubt about what came first.

"There are a lot of my blue-and-yellow buoys out there, and you and I have got to get them all," Alfred said.

It wasn't long before Sam spotted one. He called up to Alfred, who swung the boat around sharply.

There was a rope attached to the buoy, and a lobster trap at the end of the rope. When they pulled up the trap, they found three sea urchins and four crabs.

"Throw everything over the side but the big crab," Alfred said. Sam held up a small, wiggly fish. It was a baby cusk, and it too went back in. He slid the trap toward the back of the boat, washed off the coiled rope, and scrubbed the scum off the buoy. He looked out to sea again.

They picked up three more traps. Each trap held three lobsters.

"Into the box," Alfred said. "Measure them, clean them up, and off we go."

Sam held the metal ruler up to each lobster, between the claws and tail. If that space was under three inches or over five, the lobster went back in. Alfred showed Sam how to rubber-band the big claws for safety sake, and how to recognize a female with eggs.

"She's got to go back in and hatch those babies," he said.

Then they had some lunch and took off again.

They had three good days and one squally one, and suddenly the traps were all in.

"We've done it!" Alfred said. "And you are the best helper I've ever had."

They stacked the traps on the dock. Alfred went to get the truck. Sam sat down to wait and fell asleep.

BE CAREFUL OF FIRE
NOTICE
VISIT THE ISLAND
MUSEUM
MAP OF
PLEASE DO NOT PICK OUR WILD
PIZZA
STAY AT THE INN
THE BEST

They loaded the traps onto the truck and up the hill they went. As they passed the store, Sam waved to Heather and Hamilton. At Sam's house Alfred paid him, thanked him, and drove off. Sam ate supper and went right to bed.

In the morning Heather and Jonathan picked Sam up. Kenny, a summer visitor, was with them. At the field there was lots of action. Everyone was busy cleaning and decorating. Sam was to start the game in left field. Kenny had been pitching in the practice games, and he was going to have his chance.

PORT
ELCO

It was lonely out in left field. Not one hit came Sam's way. They were trailing Port Hyde in the fifth inning. Kenny was in deep trouble. They moved Sam into the pitcher's box. Sam did his best, and they won the game.

On their way to the farewell party for the Port Hyde team, Kate said, "You were great, Sam. You saved the day."

There was a reporter for the *Port Hyde Courier* on the dock.

"You've got talent," she told Sam. "Do you want a career in sports when you grow up?"

Sam thought for a few seconds. "I guess in the summer I want to play baseball, in the fall I want to go to Arizona and work in a rodeo, and in the winter I want to be a lobsterman."

And that's the way it appeared in the *Port Hyde Courier.*

ISLAND SPA
GIFTS & POST CARDS
THE COURIER IS HERE